DEPAOLA

LA·FAMILIA·MERCADO

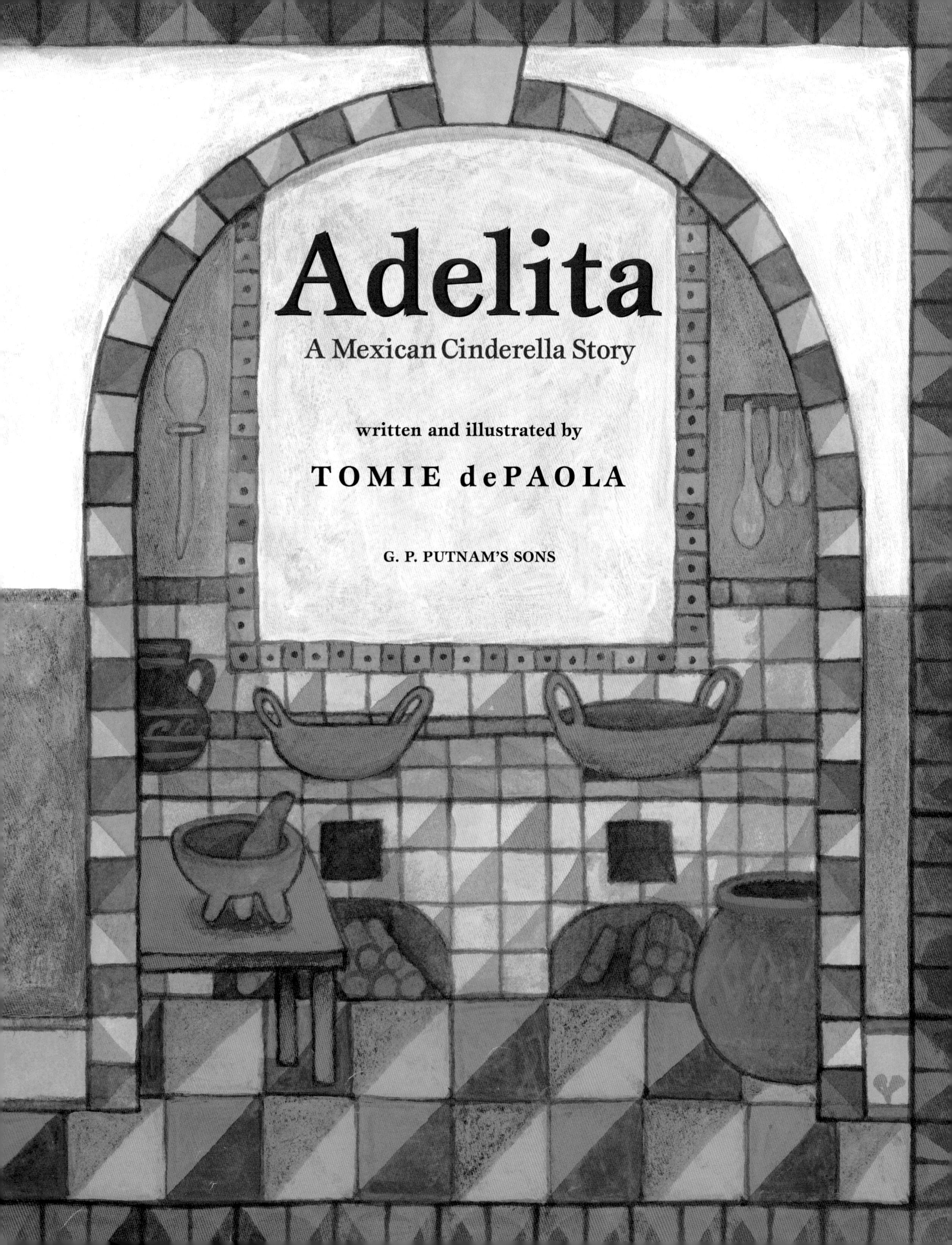

Adelita

A Mexican Cinderella Story

written and illustrated by

TOMIE dePAOLA

G. P. PUTNAM'S SONS

Hace mucho tiempo—a long time ago—in a village in Mexico, there lived a merchant named Francisco and his beautiful young wife, Adela.

One day, Adela said, "Francisco, *estamos esperando un bebé*—we are going to have a baby."

"Adela!" Francisco said. "*Me hace muy feliz saberlo*—I am so happy."

Then he said, "We must send for Esperanza. She will come and take care of you until the baby is born. And then she will help us with the baby." Esperanza had been with the Mercado family since she was a young girl, and she had looked after Francisco when he was a baby.

Esperanza came right away. She took good care of Adela, but after the birth of the baby, Adela was ill. She grew weaker, and shortly after, she held her little girl for the first and last time. Quietly, she died.

Francisco was heartbroken. He named his baby daughter Adelita—little Adela, after her mother. Francisco was sad for his Adela and he missed her greatly, but gradually Adelita filled his heart with love.

Time passed, and Adelita grew into a beautiful young woman. *La casa Mercado se llenó de alegría*—the Mercado house was full of happiness.

One evening, Francisco called Adelita and Esperanza to his study.

"My dear Adelita, my good Esperanza, *les tengo noticias*—I have some news for you. I have met a charming woman and I have decided to marry again. Her name is Señora Micaela de la Fortuna. She is a widow and has two daughters close to your age, Adelita. I know you will like Doña Micaela and her daughters, Valentina and Dulce."

Adelita was happy for her father. Esperanza wasn't so sure—especially after she met Doña Micaela and her daughters. *"Que frías son*—they're cold ones," Esperanza said.

Life was happy, but different. Adelita had to share her father's attention, but they still managed to have *importantes momentos juntos*—special moments together. Adelita didn't mind that Doña Micaela favored her daughters, even though Esperanza complained.

"*Es natural*—it's natural," Adelita told her.

Then suddenly her father died from an illness, and everything changed.

Poor Adelita was an orphan. Doña Micaela had always been jealous of Adelita. Now she no longer had to hide it. She moved Adelita from her beautiful bedroom to a small room in the attic. No longer did Adelita have new dresses. She had to wear hand-me-downs. Worst of all, Valentina and Dulce were mean and hateful to her.

Adelita began spending all her time in the kitchen with Esperanza. She helped her with the meals. She listened to stories about her father as a boy and her mother as a young bride. Because she knew that Esperanza loved her, Adelita's heart stayed as warm as the fire in the hearth.

One day, Doña Micaela came to the kitchen and spoke to them. "I am spending too much money in this household. From now on, you, Adelita, will work in the kitchen. You are here all the time anyway. And you, Esperanza—out! I want you to leave immediately."

"Oh, Señora de la Fortuna, please, don't send me away," Esperanza pleaded. "I have been with this family since I was a girl. I will work for no money, just for a place to lay my head and a bowl of beans and a tortilla."

"Oh, please, Mamá," Adelita begged. "Esperanza can share my room—and my food."

"Out!" shouted Señora Micaela de la Fortuna to Esperanza.

Then, in an icy voice, she spoke to Adelita. "And don't you dare call me *MAMÁ* again! I am Doña Micaela to you." She turned and left, nose in the air.

Entre lágrimas y abrazos—amid tears and hugs—poor Esperanza said good-bye to Adelita and left with her meager belongings.

Adelita was in despair. The days ahead held nothing but loneliness and hard work. Adelita had to prepare all the meals, clean the rooms, and fetch and carry for Valentina and Dulce, who became more like *maldad y vinagre*—meanness and vinegar.

is hijas—my daughters," Doña Micaela said one morning as ta was serving breakfast, "el Señor and la Señora Gordillo have s an invitation to *una fiesta en su hacienda*—a party at their ranch— ebrate the homecoming of their son, Javier."

"OOOOOH, Mamá," Valentina and Dulce twittered.

"And," Doña Micaela said with a smile, "*se rumora*—rumor has it— that he will be looking for a wife!"

The daughters nearly fainted. Secretly, each wanted to be the wife of Javier. And each would do anything to get him.

"Doña Micaela," Adelita asked as she poured the hot chocolate, "may I go, too? I knew Señor Javier when we were young. I would love to see him again."

"Are you serious?" Doña Micaela asked. "Look at you! So poorly dressed—such a dirty face. I would be too embarrassed to have you in our company. You will stay here. *¡Y punto!*—that is final!"

Adelita went back to the kitchen.

The next days were busy. Adelita did not have a minute to herself —washing, pressing, sewing ribbons on, taking lace off, at the mercy of every little *capricho*—whim—of the sisters as each tried to outdo the other.

So, when Doña Micaela, Valentina and Dulce left for the *fiesta,* Adelita went to the kitchen and sat by the fire. Suddenly, disappointment swept over her, and she began to weep. She missed her father. She missed Esperanza. She missed being at the *fiesta*.

Tap, tap, tap. She heard a soft knock at the door.

"Who is it?" Adelita asked.

"*Soy yo*—only me." It was Esperanza!

"Oh, Esperanza, I have missed you so much!" Adelita cried.

"Don't cry, *mi pequeñita*—my little one," Esperanza said. "I am here. I had *un sueño*—a dream—that Doña Micaela would not let you go to the *fiesta*, so I have come to help. I have borrowed a cart to take you there."

"But I have nothing to wear," Adelita said.

"Come with me," Esperanza said.

They went to the *cuarto de tiliches*—storeroom. "Over there, behind those boxes, is your mother's trunk. The key is behind the crucifix."

Adelita unlocked the trunk. Inside she found an old-fashioned, beautiful white dress. Under the dress was a magnificent *rebozo*—shawl—embroidered with birds and flowers. "Oh, *mi mamacita*—my little mother," Adelita whispered.

Adelita washed and dressed. Esperanza braided her hair and wound ribbons and flowers into it. "Oh, Esperanza," Adelita said, "Doña Micaela will be furious when she sees me!"

"Don't worry. She will never recognize you," Esperanza assured her. "Now, *¡vámonos!*—let's hurry!"

The *fiesta* had already begun when Adelita arrived. She walked into the room. Everyone turned to look. The room fell silent. Who was this stunning young woman?

Señor Gordillo went up to Adelita. "Who do we have here?" he asked.

"I'm in disguise," Adelita said with a twinkle and a sweet smile. "Just call me *Cenicienta*—Cinderella."

"Javier, everyone," Señor Gordillo said. "Come meet our very own *Cenicienta*!"

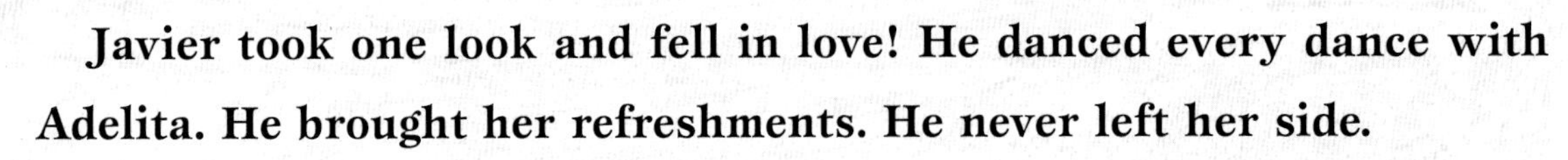

Javier took one look and fell in love! He danced every dance with Adelita. He brought her refreshments. He never left her side.

Adelita's heart was full as well, and all the meanness she had suffered over the years began to melt.

But at midnight, when Javier gave her a sweet kiss and declared his love, Adelita was frightened. How could she explain who she was? His family would never allow him to love a kitchen maid!

So Adelita ran away and found Esperanza. They hurried home.

"I will never forget this night as long as I live, Esperanza," Adelita said. "*Gracias*—thank you!"

"If you ever need me, *mi'jita*—my little daughter—just call my name and somehow I will hear you," Esperanza told her.

The next day, all Doña Micaela and her two daughters could talk about was "the mysterious *Cenicienta*" who had appeared and then disappeared from the *fiesta*, just like the fairy tale. They were jealous of her beauty and even more jealous because they knew that Javier had fallen in love with her.

"I'm glad no one knows who she is," Valentina said.

"Or where she is," Dulce said.

"And no *zapatilla de cristal*—glass slipper!" Doña Micaela added.

Javier had told everyone that he would not rest until he found his *Cenicienta*.

"He is coming to town *hoy mismísimo*—this very day," Doña Micaela announced. "He will stop at each house and look for her. This is a chance to show once more what charms you have, my daughters, so prepare yourselves. Who knows, maybe one of you will make him forget this *Cenicienta*."

"Adelita," they screamed, "come help us, quickly."

"I will be right there," Adelita answered. But before she went to Valentina and Dulce, she ran to her attic room and hung her mother's *rebozo* out the window.

She helped the two sisters dress. Then she went back to her room and shyly peeked out the window.

Soon, she saw Javier coming down the street on his horse. Suddenly, he saw the *rebozo*. He jumped down, ran to the door and knocked.

Señora Micaela de la Fortuna opened the door.

"Ah, Señor Javier! *Pásele, por favor*—come in, please," she said.

"Señora, where is she? I know my love is here," Javier said.

"Do you mean one of my daughters?" Doña Micaela said. "Valentina, Dulce, come here. Señor Javier would like to see you!"

The sisters appeared in the doorway, giggling foolishly.

"*Buen día*—good day—Señor Javier," they chimed in unison. "Do you remember us? Are you looking for us?"

"Yes, ladies, I remember you," Javier answered, "but it's another that I'm looking for."

"There's no one else here," Doña Micaela said.

"Yes, there is," a voice said. "Are you looking for me, Señor?"

There was Adelita, standing at the top of the stairs in her mother's dress and *rebozo*.

"My *Cenicienta*," Javier said.

"Who—what—what's going on?" Doña Micaela asked, while Valentina and Dulce looked at Adelita in astonishment.

"It's only Adelita, Doña Micaela," Adelita said as she came down the stairs. "Only Adelita."

"Who are you?" Javier asked.

"I am Adelita Mercado Martínez. We knew each other when we were children."

"Oh, Adelita, of course. I remember you as a little girl," Javier gasped. "I am so happy to have found you again." He smiled. "I have come to ask my *Cenicienta* to marry me. Will you?"

"I am an orphan, Señor Javier," Adelita said. "Perhaps you should ask Doña Micaela if she will give her permission."

"Will you, Señora?" Javier asked.

"Why, I don't know—I don't know what—I mean—well, of course. We shall be honored, Señor Javier," Doña Micaela said. Valentina and Dulce glared at Adelita.

"Then it will be," Javier said, taking Adelita's hand in his.

In her sweetness, Adelita invited Señora Micaela de la Fortuna Mercado and her daughters, Valentina and Dulce, to the wedding. Of course, Esperanza was there, too. She was going to take care of Javier and Adelita just as she had done before.

"And just like *Cenicienta* and her *Príncipe*—Prince—we shall live *muy felices por siempre*—happily ever after—too!" Javier said.

And they did.

Spanish Phrases

Hace mucho tiempo (HAH-seh MOO-cho tee-EM-po): A long time ago

Estamos esperando un bebé (ess-TAH-mohs ess-peh-RAHN-do oohn beh-BEH): We are going to have a baby

Me hace muy feliz saberlo (mey HAH-seh mooie feh-LEEZ sah-BARE-low): I am so happy to know (it)

La casa se llenó de alegría (lah CAH-sah seh yeh-NOH deh ah-leh-GREE-yah): The house was full of happiness

Les tengo noticias (less TEN-go no-tee-SEE-yass): I have some news

Que frías son (keh FREE-yass sohn): They're cold ones

Importantes momentos juntos (im-poor-TAHN-tess moe-MEN-tohs HOON-tohs): Special moments together

Es natural (ess nah-too-RAHL): It's natural

Entre lágrimas y abrazos (EN-treh LAH-gree-mahs ee ah-BRAH-zohs): Amid tears and hugs

Maldad y vinagre (MAHL-dahd ee vee-nah-GREH): Meanness and vinegar

Mis hijas (mees HEE-hahs): My daughters

Una fiesta en su hacienda (OO-nah fee-YES-tah ehn soo hah-see-EN-dah): A party at their ranch

Se rumora (seh roo-MORE-ah): Rumor has it

¡Y punto! (ee POON-toe): That is final!

Capricho (cah-PREE-choe): Whim

Soy yo (soi yoh): Only me

Mi pequeñita (mee peh-keh-NEE-tah): My little one

Un sueño (oohn SWAIN-yoh): A dream

Cuarto de tiliches (coo-ARE-toh deh tee-LEE-ches): Storeroom

Rebozo (ray-BOH-zoh): Shawl

Mi mamacita (mee mah-mah-SEE-tah): My little mother

¡Vámonos! (VAH-mo-nohs) Let's hurry (let's go)!

Cenicienta (seh-nee-see-EN-tah): Cinderella

Gracias (GRAH-see-ahs): Thank you

Mi'jita (mee HEE-tah): My little daughter

Zapatilla de cristal (zah-pah-TEE-yah deh cree-STAHL) Glass slipper

Hoy mismísimo (OI meez-MEE-see-moe): This very day

Pásele, por favor (PAH-seh-leh, poor fah-VOOR): Come in, please

Buen día (bwen DEE-ah): Good day

Príncipe (PREEN-see-peh): Prince

Muy felices por siempre (mooie feh-LEE-ses poor see-EM-preh): Happily ever after

 Published simultaneously in Canada. Printed in Hong Kong by South China Printing Co. (1988) Ltd. Book designed by Cecilia Yung and Gina DiMassi. Text set in Esprit Bold. The art was done in acrylics on 140 lb. Arches handmade cold-pressed watercolor paper. Library of Congress Cataloging-in-Publication Data De Paola, Tomie. Adelita: a Mexican Cinderella story / Tomie dePaola. p. cm. Summary: After the death of her mother and father, Adelita is badly mistreated by her stepmother and stepsisters until she finds her own true love at a grand fiesta. [1. Fairy tales. 2. Folklore—Mexico.] I. Title. PZ8.D437 Ad 2002 398.2'0972'02—dc21 2001057873

ISBN 0-399-23866-2 10 9 8 7 6 5 4 3 2 1

FIRST IMPRESSION